THE VOYAGE OF THE CLIPPER SHIP

RAINBIRD

FROM NEW YORK TO CALIFORNIA

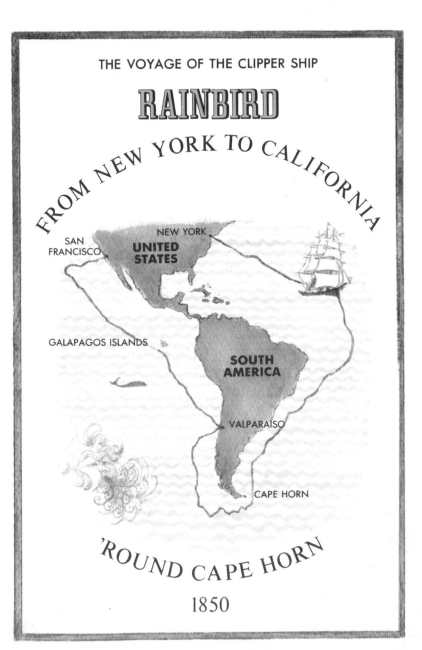

'ROUND CAPE HORN

1850

An I Can Read Book®

CLIPPER SHIP

BY
THOMAS P. LEWIS

Pictures by
JOAN SANDIN

HarperTrophy
A Division of HarperCollins*Publishers*

For Abigail, Peter and Emily T. L.

and

for Fran and Bob J. S.

HarperCollins®, ☫®, and I Can Read™ are
trademarks of HarperCollins Publishers Inc.

Clipper Ship
Text copyright © 1978 by Thomas P. Lewis
Illustrations copyright © 1978 by Joan Sandin
For information address HarperCollins
Children's Books, a division of HarperCollins Publishers,
10 East 53rd Street, New York, NY 10022.

Library of Congress Cataloging-in-Publication Data
Lewis, Thomas P.
    Clipper ship.

    (An I can read history book)
    Summary: Captain Murdock is aided by his wife
and children as he commands a clipper ship from New
York to San Francisco.
    [1. Clipper ships—Fiction]   I. Sandin, Joan.
II. Title.
PZ7.L5882Cl   [E]   77-11858
ISBN 0-06-023808-9
ISBN 0-06-023809-7 (lib. bdg.)
ISBN 0-06-444160-1 (pbk.)

First Harper Trophy edition, 1992.

The *Rainbird* sailed away
from New York Harbor,
bound for California.

Captain Murdock stood by the wheel

giving orders to the crew.

Mrs. Murdock stood beside him.

"Pray for good weather, Mary Elizabeth,"

the captain said. "It would be good

to beat the *White Cloud*."

Jamie and Meg said good-bye
to their home in New York.
"Maybe we will find gold in California,"
said Meg.

"I hope we do," said Jamie.
"I would like to have a gold watch."

Three days out.

The passengers unpack their things
and walk the decks.

"Look!" says one. "A school of dolphins."

"I feel sick," says another.

"I must go below."

Some of the crew climb the masts.

"A bully mate and a captain, too,"
they sing.

They crawl out on the yards
and let out more sail.

"Doo-da, doo-da day!

Around Cape Horn to Frisco Bay!"

8

The crew check the cargo below.

There are tools and stoves
and weather vanes, bushels of grain,
bolts of cloth, and many other things.
There are two thousand
red handkerchiefs to sell in California.

One of the sailors has a parrot.

The parrot begins to sneeze.

"God bless you!" says the sailor.

In the captain's cabin
Mrs. Murdock studies the charts
while Jamie looks on.
The cabin is their home.

There is Meg's bunk and
there is Jamie's.
Jamie keeps his telescope
in the hammock by his pillow.
There is Mrs. Murdock's chronometer,
the sextant, and sheets of paper
filled with figures.
"With a good northeast breeze,"
says Mrs. Murdock,
"we should pass Bermuda tonight."

Up on deck
Meg draws pictures of the dolphins.

13

Each day is different.

Sometimes the wind is light.

The crew mend sails,

wash the decks, and polish brass.

The passengers play cards
and read their books.

Captain Murdock looks the ship over
from bow to stern.

He teaches Jamie about the *Rainbird*.

Sometimes the day is dark.

Then, how alone they seem

on the great black sea.

16

One day a storm arises.

The passengers go to their cabins

as the sea crashes down upon the ship.

"Climb the rigging!"

the captain orders.

"Reef the topsails!

Furl the courses!"

The men are afraid.

The captain shouts again.

"Climb up, boys! Take in sail!"

The sea comes over the bow

and washes down the decks.

Captain Murdock takes the wheel
and holds the *Rainbird* steady on course.

"Man overboard!"

cries the mate.

One of the sailors

has fallen from the rigging.

"Alas, the poor soul is lost,"

says a sailor.

The captain brings the *Rainbird* around

to look for the missing sailor.

Mrs. Murdock studies

the direction of the wind

and the way the current is flowing.

"Sail south by southwest,"

she says to her husband.

"Now sail west!

There he is now, poor fellow."

"Lower the boat!" the captain cries.

The men row through the high waves.

They pull the half-drowned man

into the boat.

Then they row back

as hard as they can.

They wrap the man in blankets.

Mrs. Murdock gives him rum to drink.

"Thank you, ma'am,"

the sailor says.

Mrs. Murdock smiles.

"Why, you're welcome, mister."

The children smile too.

The *Rainbird* crosses the equator.

The sun is hot.

The sailors take off their shirts.

Some of the passengers do too.

Other passengers are shocked!

"*That* is not proper," they say.

Meg and Jamie climb one of the masts

to look at the equator.

But all they can see is ocean.

"Meg! Jamie!" their mother calls.

"It is time for your lessons."

"In a minute, Mother," says Jamie.

Through his telescope

he has seen a whale breach.

Meg sees it too.

But she is busy

making curls in her hair.

She rolls her hair around bits of rag

and ties them in knots.

"Come *now*, children,"

says their mother.

Meg and Jamie come down.

Their mother teaches them

how to read and write,

how to add and subtract.

Then she tells them stories

about what it was like

when she was growing up.

Cape Horn is at the very end
of South America.

Here there is an island called
Tierra del Fuego,
which means "Land of Fire."
There is nothing to see
but ice and snow,
penguins and whales.
Here the Atlantic Ocean
meets the Pacific Ocean.
Here the winds blow very hard.
Some ships sink.
The *Rainbird* begins to tremble.

28

Through the portholes of their cabins
the people see icebergs.

Captain Murdock says a prayer.

"Please be to God, we will all be safe.

Please, God, be good to the ship.

Amen."

Just then the *Rainbird* meets a wave.

Meg's plate flies off the table

onto her lap!

"I feel sick, Mary Elizabeth,"
the captain says.

"Meg—Jamie—fetch the doctor,"
says the captain's wife.

The doctor looks at the captain.

"It is brain fever," he says.

"You must go to bed."

"But who will sail the ship?"
asks Captain Murdock.

"I will sail the ship,"

says Mrs. Murdock.

It is the middle of July

and it is snowing.

It is winter at Cape Horn.

The sea is white with ice and foam.

The *Rainbird* sails through the water

like a great wooden fish.

Mrs. Murdock watches out for icebergs

and keeps the ship

away from the Land of Fire.

She tries to find a safe place

for the *Rainbird* to go.

She orders studding sails

on the larboard booms.

Meg and Jamie watch their mother.

They have tied themselves

to the deck with ropes

to keep from falling into the sea.

A sail tears loose!

It falls to the deck.

The men hold fast and pray

as the *Rainbird* sails around the Horn.

36

Many days pass.

The ship is safe now,

but some of the passengers are sick.

The captain is still in bed

because the fever is so bad.

"Hello, Father," says Jamie.

"I have looked us over

from bow to stern.

Everything is all right

except for some spars and sails

that are broken."

"Good morning, Papa," says Meg.

"I have drawn you pictures

of birds that I have seen."

"Birds?" says the captain.

"We must be close to shore."

The *Rainbird* puts in
at the city of Valparaiso, Chile.
She repairs a cracked bowsprit
and some lost spars and sails.
Then she heads back to sea.

41

When the sea is quiet,

Meg and Jamie help their mother.

They steer the ship

north, north to California.

"Maybe," says Jamie, "with the money
we make from the voyage
I will buy *two* gold watches."
"I would like to see
the old Spanish missions," says Meg.
"And send a letter home."

The *Rainbird* anchors in the harbor
of a small island in the Pacific.

She takes on fresh water,
fruits, and vegetables.
The passengers look at the natives
and the natives look at them.

One of the natives gives them a head
as a present to show they are friends.
"Blow me down!" says the mate.
"It is a *human* head!"

Later, the *Rainbird* passes
the Galápagos Islands.
She does not stop,
so the children cannot see
the giant tortoises that live there.

Another ship passes the *Rainbird*

on the way to California.

She is the *White Cloud,*

one of the fastest ships

that sail the seas.

The *Rainbird* puts on full sail,

but still she cannot catch her.

The *White Cloud* is

like a lovely white bird

flying over the ocean.

"How beautiful," says Mrs. Murdock.

"Still, I should have liked

to overtake her."

Meg and Jamie watch
until the *White Cloud* is out of sight.

Night is a special time at sea.

The children know all the stars.

Meg has no need of Jamie's telescope.

She makes a better one with her hand.

Jamie, restless,

makes a blowgun with his hand

and shoots a piece of

ship's tar at Cook.

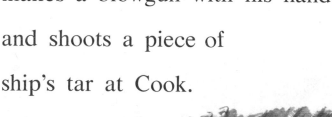

Captain Murdock sits up in his bed

and he, too, looks out

at the beautiful sky.

Jamie and Meg

play hide-and-seek in the hold.

50

Jamie hides behind a case of blankets,

but Meg finds him.

Meg hides behind a barrel of nails.

But the parrot gives her away.

He likes to stand on her shoulder.

When it is calm,

the longboats pull the *Rainbird*

in search of a fresh wind.

The men can see sharks in the water.

"Skee-daddle, fish!" a sailor says.

Then the winds begin to blow.

The sails of the *Rainbird* fill out.

She has dozens of sails

which pull her through the sea.

She sweeps through the ocean

with all her sails flying.

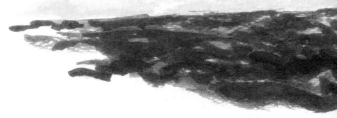

The *Rainbird* sails on
to San Francisco, California.
The bay is filled with other ships
as the *Rainbird* makes her way in.

Captain Murdock
is almost well now.
He comes on deck
to stand by his wife.
Together they bring their ship
to the very streets of the city.
They wave to other captains
and to the people on shore.
The word spreads quickly
that the *Rainbird* has two captains.

"Mary Elizabeth,"

says Captain Murdock to his wife,

"I am proud of you."

"And I of you,"

says Mrs. Murdock.

Jamie and Meg show the *Rainbird*
to people from the city.
Jamie trades his telescope
for two gold watches.
"Someday," says Meg,
"I would like to live in California
and see the mountains."

They say good-bye to the passengers.

They shake the hands of the crew.

"I hope," says Captain James
to the crew, "to see you all again
to make the passage home."

"Aye, sir!" says the mate.
"That is, some of us will.
Some will stay in California
to look for gold."
Captain Murdock smiles and nods.

He and Mrs. Murdock,

Meg, and Jamie

have dinner on shore.

They talk about their journey.

They raise their glasses

in a toast to one another.

"Here's to Meg! Here's to Jamie!"

"Here's to Mother! Here's to Father!"

Then the two captains of the *Rainbird*
toast each other with a kiss.

AUTHOR'S NOTE

The story of the *Rainbird* is based on tales of clipper ship voyages around 1850, following the discovery of gold in California. If the winds were fair, the voyage from New York Harbor to San Francisco Bay would take about three months. It is also based on the true-life stories of Mary Patten, Mrs. Charlotte Babcock, Mrs. Cressy, Mrs. Clark, and many other women who went to sea with their husbands and families.

Some families spent many years at sea. The McColm family, for example, lived on board ship for thirteen years. When they retired, their two sons were quite astonished by life on shore—they had never lived in a house.